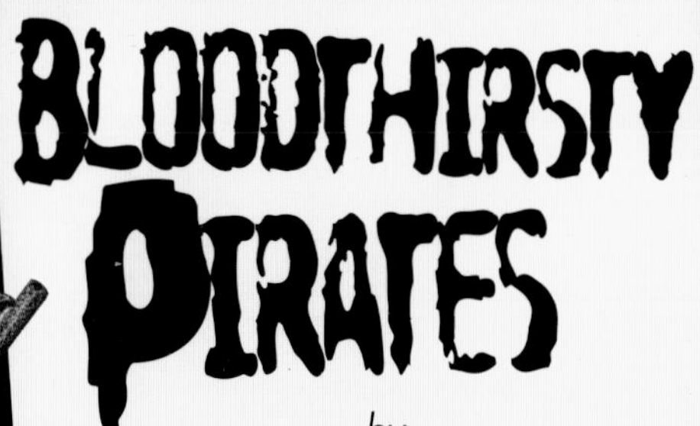

by

Richard Mead

A Long Story

Long John Silver was the sly and treacherous pirate created by Robert Louis Stevenson for his book *Treasure Island*. Today, stories about pirates continue to be as popular as ever.

THIEVES ABOARD!

Bold, adventurous, and often bloodthirsty, pirates terrorized the seas for thousands of years. These oceangoing robbers plundered ships for treasure, hoping for great rewards. But life as a pirate was never easy....

TREASURE ISLAND

In the sixteenth century, major trade routes opened up between Europe and the Far East. Ships laden with gold and silver sailed the Indian Ocean, offering rich pickings for pirates. The island of Madagascar, situated off the east coast of Africa, was an ideal base for hunting out passing trade ships. It became a pirate kingdom that, at one time, attracted around 1,500 pirates!

KEEPING THE CODE

Life at sea offered certain freedoms, but pirates couldn't always do whatever they wanted. Most ships had their own code of conduct that the crew had to obey. The code often included rules about gambling and also banned women from going aboard the boat!

Food supplies often ran low. In 1670, Henry Morgan's crew of pirates had to eat roasted leather satchels!

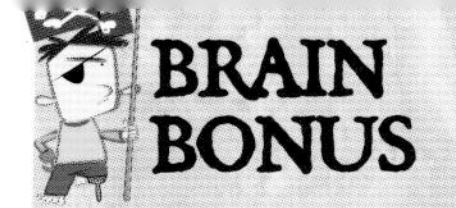

BRAIN BONUS

What was hardtack?

a) a biscuit
b) a punishment
c) a part of the sail

Which of these is a symptom of scurvy?

a) sore gums
b) hair loss
c) blurry vision

Black Bart had salmagundi on the day he died. What is it?

a) a vegetable
b) a type of wine
c) a favorite pirate meal from the West Indies

(answers on page 32)

SCURVY KNAVES

A pirate's diet was not a healthy one. Food and water would quickly spoil on long voyages. Without vitamin C, found in fresh fruits and vegetables, pirates were likely to get a disease called scurvy. Pirates often ate limes, which are rich in vitamin C, to prevent scurvy.

Lime

POPULATION: ONE!

There were tough punishments for pirates who broke their ship's code. If they stole from another crew member or tried to desert the ship, they could end up marooned on an island. All they would be left with was some water and a pistol, so the chance of surviving was slim.

WARRIOR WOMEN

Most ships allowed only men on board. So for many women who wanted to sail the high seas, the only answer was to dress and act like men!

BRAIN BONUS

Where did Anne Bonny meet Jack Rackham?

a) Bahamas
b) Jamaica
c) in church

How many pirates did Ching Shih command?

a) 8,000
b) 18,000
c) 80,000

Which actress played a pirate in *Cutthroat Island*?

a) Sandra Bullock
b) Geena Davis
c) Julia Roberts

(answers on page 32)

BONNY ON BOARD

Anne Bonny became a pirate after meeting Captain Jack Rackham. Together, the pair terrorized Spanish treasure ships until they were captured in 1720. Rackham was hanged, but Anne escaped the death penalty because she was pregnant.

Anne Bonny

READ ON!

Mary Read disguised herself as a man to join Jack Rackham's pirate crew. As the picture shows, her victims were amazed when they discovered she was a woman. Read was a fearless fighter—when Rackham's ship was captured by the British navy, she and Anne Bonny were the only pirates who fought back.

PIRATE PRINCESS

A Scandinavian princess called Alwilda became a pirate to avoid marrying a Danish prince. When the prince was sent to bring her back, she was so impressed by his fighting skills that she agreed to marry him!

BERRY FIERCE!

Charlotte De Berry joined the British navy, pretending to be a man. When she was attacked by her captain, she led a mutiny against him and cut off his head. Charlotte took command, and the crew became pirates.

SHIH'S IN CHARGE

In the nineteenth century, a woman named Ching Shih inherited a huge pirate empire from her husband. At one point, she controlled a fleet of 1,800 boats that terrorized the coast of China. When Ching Shih surrendered, thousands of her men switched sides and joined the Chinese navy.

Mary Read

BRAIN BONUS

The Greeks used triremes against pirates. What were these?

a) catapults
b) spears
c) warships

Which of these was a famous Viking pirate?

a) Sweyn Forkbeard
b) Gunthar Knifenose
c) Harald Spoonface

What does the word "viking" mean?

a) to sail quickly
b) to go on a sea raid
c) to destroy by fire

(answers on page 32)

PREMIER PIRATES

Piracy has a long history—it even features in ancient Greek art and writing. In the first century B.C., pirates were a menace to Roman trade. Hundreds of years later, in northern Europe, Viking warriors plundered the seas.

SEA CHANGE

In one ancient Greek myth, the god of wine, Dionysus, was captured by pirates. The angry god transformed himself into a lion, and his frightened captors hurled themselves into the sea, where they were turned into dolphins!

Julius Caesar

RANSOMED ROMAN

Before he became Roman emperor, Julius Caesar was captured by pirates. In 78 B.C., he was held hostage on a tiny island for over six weeks until the ransom had been paid. After he was released, he returned with a group of soldiers and killed all of his kidnappers.

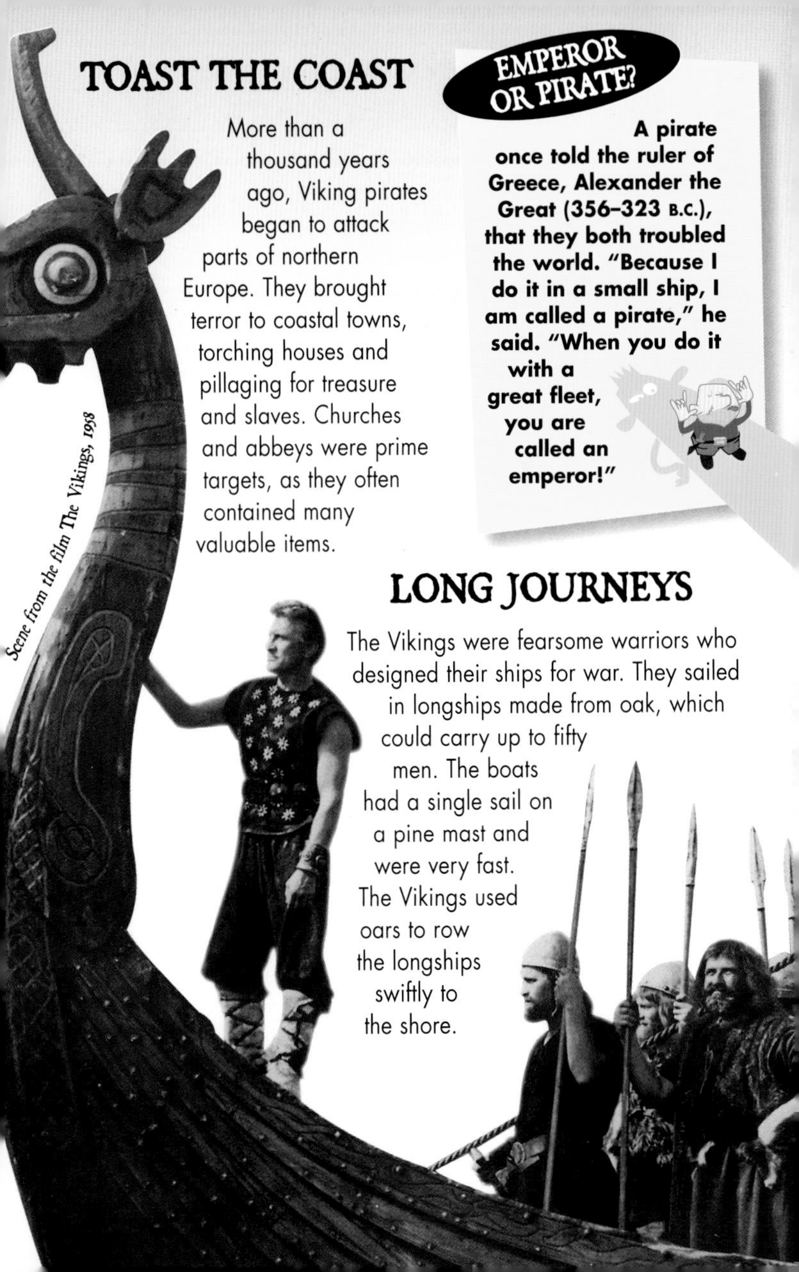

TOAST THE COAST

More than a thousand years ago, Viking pirates began to attack parts of northern Europe. They brought terror to coastal towns, torching houses and pillaging for treasure and slaves. Churches and abbeys were prime targets, as they often contained many valuable items.

EMPEROR OR PIRATE?

A pirate once told the ruler of Greece, Alexander the Great (356–323 B.C.), that they both troubled the world. "Because I do it in a small ship, I am called a pirate," he said. "When you do it with a great fleet, you are called an emperor!"

LONG JOURNEYS

The Vikings were fearsome warriors who designed their ships for war. They sailed in longships made from oak, which could carry up to fifty men. The boats had a single sail on a pine mast and were very fast. The Vikings used oars to row the longships swiftly to the shore.

Scene from the film *The Vikings*, 1958

Cog ship

LEAGUE LEADERS

In the Middle Ages, pirates tormented shipping on the Baltic Sea in northern Europe. Some German merchants banded together and designed a new ship called a cog. With a fortified bow (front) and stern (back) and high sides, it was a difficult vessel to board!

BRAIN BONUS

How many cannons did Spanish galleons usually carry?

a) 12
b) 30
c) 60

What is a rudder used for?

a) hoisting the sail
b) pumping out seawater
c) steering the ship

How many rowers powered a galley?

a) 300
b) 3,000
c) 30

(answers on page 32)

STRENGTH IN NUMBERS

In the sixteenth century, Spanish ships known as galleons were used to carry treasure to Europe from North and South America. But these heavy ships were hard to defend and were easy pickings for pirates. To protect their booty, galleons traveled in convoys of up to 100 ships.

A LOAD OF JUNKS

Pirate junks were a scary sight in the Far East. They were captured cargo ships, which the pirates adapted for attacking other boats. The largest junks were around 100 feet long and could carry up to 400 men. Serious firepower was added, too—there was room for thirty cannons!

SHIP-SHAPE

Many pirates built their own attack ships or simply stole ships from their enemies. Meanwhile, their unlucky victims had to find ways to defend themselves from these bloodthirsty sea robbers.

A corsair's galley

THE RAM RAMP

In the seventeenth century, Muslim pirates, called corsairs, used a type of ship called a galley to chase after their victims. It had a battering ram at the front for smashing into the sides of enemy boats. The ram could also be used as a bridge for boarding the enemy boat.

BARNACLE BUILDUP

Cleaning a ship took more than a bucket and mop! Every few months, barnacles and seaweed had to be scraped and sometimes burned off the bottom, or hull, of the ship.

PIRATE POSSESSIONS

Pirates had a job to do, for which they had their own "tools of the trade." Besides weapons for fighting, they also needed tools for building and repairing their ships, and of course, clothes to wear!

FANCY DRESS?

Real pirates didn't look like the ones we see in the movies. Their clothes were tattered and they never bathed. The only time they got wet was when they jumped into the sea! They certainly wouldn't have kept a parrot as a pet—they'd probably have eaten it instead!

BRAIN BONUS

What is a dirk?

a) an ax
b) a dagger
c) a gun

Which of these is part of a pistol's firing mechanism?

a) frizzen
b) blixen
c) quassle

Why was brass used to make guns?

a) It was very cheap.
b) It doesn't rust.
c) It's very light.

(answers on page 32)

SECONDHAND

Pirates' weapons were often stolen from their victims. In the seventeenth century, the cutlass was very popular. With its short blade, this sword was easy to swing in the close quarters onboard ship. Daggers—sharp pointed knives—could be hidden in clothes for surprise attacks.

Long John Silver

FIGHTING FUND

Pirates injured in battle usually received compensation from the captain. Losing a finger was worth about 100 pieces of silver, while a leg could be worth eight times as much.

TOOL TIME

Boatbuilding was a complicated process. A tool called an adze was used to shape and smooth wood planks. The gaps or seams between the planks were filled with rope fibers called oakum, then sealed with tar to keep water from seeping in. After the boat was put to sea, leaks were repaired by hammering new oakum into the seams with a caulking iron.

PISTOL PROBLEMS

Guns were popular weapons with pirates—from long-range muskets to smaller pistols. But they weren't always useful. When the sea was choppy, aiming guns accurately could be difficult. Reloading took a long time, so pirates often used a gun's butt to bash enemies over the head!

Antique pistol

BRAIN BONUS

When is the earliest record of the name *Jolly Roger* being used?

a) 1699
b) 1724
c) 1741

Black and white pirate flags became known as...

a) blackjollies
b) jollyjacks
c) blackjacks

Why did some Chinese pirates put bats on their flags?

a) to bring good luck
b) to frighten other sailors
c) to scare birds away from food supplies

(answers on page 32)

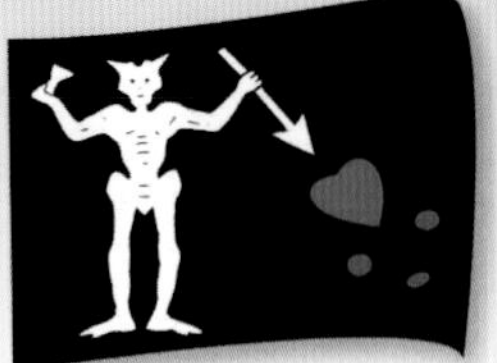

HAVE A HEART

Blackbeard was one of the most terrifying pirates of all time. His flag showed the figure of a skeleton. In one hand, the skeleton is aiming an arrow at a bleeding heart. In the other, it is holding an hourglass. Sailors knew their time had run out when they saw this symbol!

CHEERS!

English-born Bartholomew Roberts (Black Bart) became a pirate around 1720. His Jolly Roger featured himself and the figure of death raising a drink. But after the governors of two Caribbean islands tried to capture him, he flew a new flag. This showed him with the skulls of inhabitants from the two islands!

FRIEND OR FOE?

Pirates sometimes misled enemy ships by flying a friendly flag or even dressing up as women! As the pirates drew close, they would suddenly raise the Jolly Roger just before they started the attack!

FLAG DAY

In the past, spotting an unfamiliar ship approaching would have made any sailor nervous. But if a ship was flying a Jolly Roger (a pirate flag), it meant that trouble was dead ahead!

Christopher Moody's flag

SKULL-DUGGERY

Pirate captains often included the skull and crossbones on their flags as a symbol of death. These designs were usually white on a black background, but not always; Christopher Moody (1694–1722) used a red background for his skull and crossbones flag.

Jack Rackham's flag

Thomas Tew's flag

Henry Avery's flag

RED ALERT

The earliest pirate flags were plain red—the color of blood—meaning no mercy would be given to enemies. The name *Jolly Roger* may have come from the French *joli rouge* (pretty red).

BRAIN BONUS

How were the two privateers Sir Francis Drake and John Hawkins related? Were they...

a) brothers-in-law?
b) cousins?
c) uncle and nephew?

Which city did privateer Jean Lafitte help to defend?

a) Boston
b) New Orleans
c) Philadelphia

In 1603, which English king canceled letters of marque?

a) Charles I
b) Henry VIII
c) James I

(answers on page 32)

LEGAL THEFT

Privateers were pirates who worked for a government. If a country was at war with another, it would license a ship-owner to attack the enemy's vessels in return for a share of the booty!

WALTER'S WOE

Sir Walter Raleigh was an English adventurer who supported privateering. He wanted to use the profits to fund a new colony in North America. Unfortunately, his plans were cut short after a voyage to find gold for King James I (1603–1625). When Raleigh returned empty-handed, the king had him beheaded.

GALLEON GOLD

Sir Francis Drake (c. 1543–1596) isn't only famous for sailing around the world and defeating the Spanish Armada (navy); he was also a privateer. Drake stole treasure worth more than $160,000 from one Spanish galleon, which he presented to Queen Elizabeth I. It's no wonder she called him "my pirate"!

Spanish treasure

FRENCH FORTUNE

French privateers made such a fortune plundering English ships that the King of France, Louis XIV (1638–1715), asked if they could lend him some money!

MARQUE MY WORDS

Licenses given to privateers were called letters of marque. These documents were also handed out in peacetime. They allowed sailors robbed at sea to attack ships from the pirates' home country—and not be charged with piracy themselves.

TRADE WAR

During the Revolutionary War (1775–1783), John Paul Jones, an officer in the American navy, attacked British merchant ships, weakening Britain's trade with America. This was called *guerre de course*. The British may have considered him a pirate, but to Americans he became a hero.

John Paul Jones

BRAIN BONUS

What were doubloons?

a) gold coins
b) rubies
c) silk trousers

How did the Spanish coins called pieces of eight get their name?

a) They had eight sides.
b) They were worth eight reals.
c) Only eight were ever made.

On which island did William Kidd bury a treasure chest?

a) Easter Island
b) Gardiner's Island
c) Isle of Man

(answers on page 32)

A ROBBER ROBBED?

A famous haul was made by the pirate Henry Avery in 1695. He captured the *Gang-i-Sawai*, a ship that belonged to the Great Mogul of India, which was carrying treasure worth $500,000. Avery then retired, although one story claims he was robbed of all his money by merchants who knew he couldn't report them!

Treasure chest

Spices

SPICE BOYS

Pirates weren't just after money and jewels. Tobacco, sugar, and some spices were valuable hauls and could be traded when the crew reached land. Food and drink were also gratefully received if supplies were low.

BURIED BOOTY

Why did people become pirates? To make their fortunes, of course! One pirate became so wealthy he even had a golden mast made for his ship.

ONE FOR YOU…

The pirates' code ruled that all treasure must be divided among the crew. However, the captain and his officers usually received a bigger share. And some captains tried to get a lot more by sailing off before the plunder had been divided up!

TEW MUCH?

In 1693, the American pirate Thomas Tew overpowered a ship returning to Bombay, India. The vessel was packed with booty, and each member of Tew's crew received a share worth $5,000. Today, that share would have been worth over 1.5 million dollars.

MISSING MONEY

It's said that Blackbeard once left one of his fourteen wives to guard a treasure chest on a desert island. Neither she nor the treasure was ever seen again!

BRAIN BONUS

What was Blackbeard's real name?

a) James Learned
b) Steven Masters
c) Edward Teach

What did Henry Avery rename his first ship?

a) *The Fancy*
b) *The Fighter*
c) *The Freedom*

What was the pirate Black Bart's favorite drink?

a) rum
b) seawater
c) tea

(answers on page 32)

MORGAN'S MISSIONS

Around 1630, pirates called buccaneers began preying on the Spanish in the Caribbean. The greatest buccaneer ever was Sir Henry Morgan. He led many daring raids on Spanish ships and colonies, returning after one voyage with 100,000 pieces of eight. King Charles II was so impressed that he made Morgan deputy governor of Jamaica.

A LIFE OF CRIME

William Kidd started off as a successful New York businessman. Then, on a business voyage, he killed a member of his crew and turned to piracy. Legend claims that he buried his Bible to show he was turning to crime!

THE ARCH WAY

Henry Avery was so infamous he was known as the archpirate. Part of a privateering expedition, he convinced the crew to mutiny and became their captain. Within a year he was a rich man and had a fleet of six ships!

Henry Avery

SUPERIOR SEA DOGS

What makes a pirate famous? The number of years he spent at sea? The amount of treasure he captured? Or perhaps it's how much he terrified people....

William Kidd

WARNING SHOT

From 1716 to 1718, Blackbeard terrorized the waters off the North American coast. He didn't just scare sailors—he had his own crew cowering, too. He shot his first mate, Israel Hands, claiming that if he didn't kill one of his crew now and then, they would forget who he was!

WHAT A BLAST!

To avoid capture, a pirate called Rahmah bin Jabr set light to the gunpowder store on his ship. He was able to destroy half of the attacking ships but blew himself up in the process.

GOING GLOBAL

From the Caribbean to the South China Sea, sailors were rarely safe from pirates. Although names and customs differed from place to place, there was always someone ready to attack....

Dao sword

HAIR TODAY...

Before he became a pirate, Chui Apoo worked as a barber in Hong Kong!

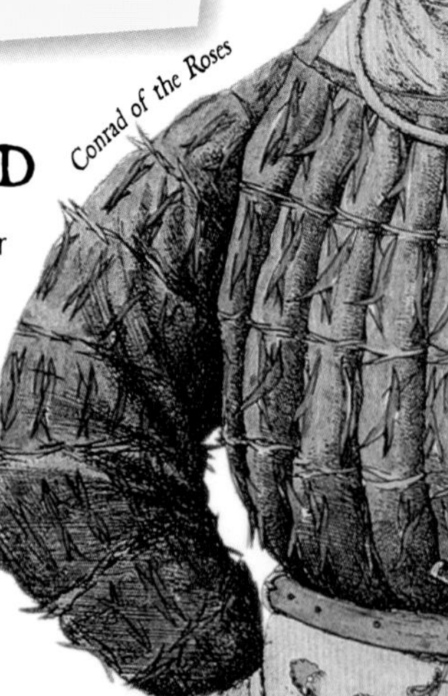

Conrad of the Roses

RED DREAD

European ships had to watch out for Muslim corsairs on the Barbary Coast. The most famous were probably Aruj and Khair ed-Din, known as the Brothers Barbarossa. But danger wasn't always so far away—Europe had plenty of its own pirates to contend with, such as the German pirate called Conrad of the Roses.

FIERCE FLEET

This is a *dao* sword, which is decorated with tufts of human hair. It was a popular weapon with pirates in Southeast Asia. One of the most feared of these pirates was Chui Apoo, who commanded over 500 vessels. But in 1849, his fleet was destroyed by British warships and, after being betrayed by his followers, he died in prison.

FIGHTING FARMERS

The Caribbean was home to the bloodthirsty buccaneers. Many were farmers whose land had been taken by the Spanish. They were joined by runaway slaves and escaped convicts. Buccaneers often dressed in animal hide, never bathed, and were famously stinky.

RAIDING ROVERS

Trade between Europe and the East meant that many boats had to pass through the Indian Ocean. The shipments of jewels, spices, and ivory encouraged pirates like the Gujarati Rovers, who spread out their boats 6 miles apart, creating a "pirate net" that was almost impossible to avoid.

BRAIN BONUS

Where is the Barbary Coast?

a) North Africa
b) Russia
c) South America

Which buccaneer once spit-roasted two farmers alive?

a) François L'Olonnois
b) Henry Morgan
c) Rock Braziliano

Where were the Barbarossa brothers born?

a) Greece
b) Morocco
c) Turkey

(answers on page 32)

BRAIN BONUS

For what purpose did pirates use a grappling iron?

a) to load a cannon
b) to pull two ships together
c) to attach the sail to the mast

Which musical instrument did Sir Francis Drake take on his voyages?

a) a drum
b) a flute
c) a violin

What were caltrops used for?

a) sharpening cutlasses
b) shouting to another ship
c) spiking the feet of enemies

(answers on page 32)

IT'S A BREEZE!

Treasure ships were often attacked at the beginning of a voyage. That's because they couldn't work up much speed until they found a strong wind to power the sails. Ships leaving the Caribbean would always head north to get a good wind, so crafty pirates would lie in wait off the American coast.

FIRE AWAY

The buccaneer Henry Morgan once found his route blocked by three Spanish warships. As a solution, he got his crew to fit a "fire ship" with fake guns and wooden sailors. It was launched toward the Spanish boats and burst into flames. Morgan escaped and even captured one of the Spanish ships!

Blackbeard

DREAD HEAD

Blackbeard's name was enough to scare the wits out of sailors, but in the flesh this fearsome pirate was even worse! He made himself look as terrifying as possible by braiding his beard into dreadlocks and tying long smoking matches under his hat.

TACTIC TIME

Pirates would quite often avoid a fight if they could. But if they did go into battle, they had plenty of clever tactics to give them the upper hand!

WHAT A DIN!

Pirates didn't just use musical instruments for entertainment. When played together, drums and wind instruments could make a real racket. This noise was a useful scare tactic when attacking treasure ships. Pirates added to the chaos by waving their cutlasses and shouting threats—enough to unnerve any enemy!

Pirates pretending to be harmless passengers

SINGLE SHOT

Privateer Jonathan Haraden once attacked a ship by standing next to a cannon, holding a burning candle. The ship surrendered, not knowing Jonathan had only one cannonball!

PIRATE PUNISHMENTS

Being a pirate had its drawbacks. If you weren't killed in battle, there was always the chance you would be caught and executed. Even your own crewmates could punish you!

BRAIN BONUS

Why did it take two attempts to hang William Kidd?

a) His crewmates attempted a rescue.
b) The first rope broke.
c) The crowd knocked the gallows over.

Which punishment involved being dragged through the water?

a) keelhauling
b) shark baiting
c) wave flogging

What did it mean to "dance the hempen jig"?

a) to get married
b) to drown at sea
c) to be hanged

(answers on page 32)

Pirate punishment

KNOT NICE

The cat-o'-nine-tails was a common punishment at sea. It was a whip made from nine cords of rope, each of which ended in a knot. To add to the torture, the sailor about to be whipped often had to make the cat-o'-nine-tails himself.

NO KIDDING!

The bodies of dead pirates were often hung in iron cages from a wooden frame called a gibbet. When William Kidd was executed in 1701, his corpse was covered in tar to stop decay and placed at the mouth of the River Thames, where it served as a warning to other sailors not to become pirates.

GIBBET GAUGE

Before he was executed, a pirate was measured to make sure he would fit in the gibbet cage, an iron cage in which his dead body would hang.

KILLING TIME

A pirate sentenced to death onboard ship faced several methods of execution. One was being made to "walk the plank" into the sea, but this was rare. Usually, condemned pirates were shot or hurled from high up in the rigging onto the deck.

Walking the plank

LOCKED UP

Privateers who were caught would often end up in prison—usually for good! Prisons were badly overcrowded and disease was common. Often, the only hope for survival was to bribe a guard for food or better conditions.

THE PIRATE POLICE

Governments couldn't just stand by and watch their ships being robbed, so they hired sailors to capture pirates—dead or alive!

BRAIN BONUS

Which pirate was once a pirate hunter?

a) Henry Avery
b) John Rackham
c) William Kidd

What was the reward for capturing the pirate Blackbeard?

a) £10
b) £100
c) £1,000

Why did William James first become a sailor?

a) to avoid a punishment for poaching
b) to sail with his grandfather
c) He was kidnapped.

(answers on page 32)

JAMES' AIMS

The Maratha pirates controlled the sea off the west coast of India in the early eighteenth century—until William James came along. In his forty-gun ship *The Protector*, James sailed close to the Maratha pirates' fort. He bombarded it for two days before it blew up.

The Swallow

HARD TO SWALLOW

The man-of-war was a heavily armed warship used by the British navy against pirates. One of these ships, *The Swallow*, helped to defeat Bartholomew Roberts (Black Bart) off the coast of West Africa. Roberts fought back but was killed by a shot in the neck.

BOAT BOMB

In 1693, the English navy tried to destroy a pirate base using a boat filled with gunpowder. Unfortunately, before reaching the base, the boat hit a rock, and so the only victim was an unlucky cat left on the boat!

MAYNARD'S MISSION

Lieutenant Robert Maynard had a tricky job—he was hired to hunt down Blackbeard! Maynard tracked down the famous pirate and fought him on the deck of his ship. Legend has it that Blackbeard received twenty cutlass wounds and five pistol shots before he died.

Duel: Blackbeard vs. Maynard

FOREIGN HUNTER

Singapore came under attack from piracy in the nineteenth century. To stamp out the problem, a $30 reward was offered for the death or capture of each pirate. Captain Farquhar of HMS *Albatross* helped to sink eighty-eight pirate boats—and earned a huge $33,000.

FICTIONAL FIGHTERS

Real or fictional, stories of pirates never fail to entertain us. Today there are numerous books, plays, and films telling tall tales about exciting adventures on the high seas.

Hook (Dustin Hoffman)

YOU'RE HOOKED

One of the most famous fictional characters is Captain Hook from the play *Peter Pan*, first staged in 1904. Created by the writer J.M. Barrie, Hook is Peter Pan's enemy and comes to a sticky end when he is eaten by a crocodile. The play eventually became a book, an animated movie, and a Steven Spielberg film.

PIRATE POETRY

Lord Byron wrote a famous poem about a pirate in 1814. It was called "The Corsair" and has since been turned into several operas and even a ballet.

PIRATES WHO PLAY

Not only do pirates show up in storybooks and on the silver screen, they can also be found on the playing field. Sports teams, like baseball's Pittsburgh Pirates and football's Tampa Bay Buccaneers, hope that their names inspire as much fear in their opponents as the Jolly Roger did in sailors long ago.

AAAH, JIM LAD!

In the book *Treasure Island*, cabin boy Jim Hawkins sails on a treasure quest, only to discover that half the crew are pirates. Author Robert Louis Stevenson based their leader, Long John Silver, on a friend who had only one leg.

FANTASTIC FLYNN

Errol Flynn was the silver screen's supreme swashbuckler. He became a star after playing a pirate in the film *Captain Blood* (1935). Famed for performing all his own stunts, Flynn also made a big splash in the 1940 film *The Sea Hawk*.

BRAIN BONUS

Who wrote the operetta *The Pirates of Penzance*?

a) Bernstein and Sondheim
b) Gilbert and Sullivan
c) Lennon and McCartney

In *Peter Pan*, how did Captain Hook lose his hand?

a) chopping vegetables
b) bitten off by a crocodile
c) cut off by Peter Pan

What was the name of Jim Hawkins' ship in *Treasure Island*?

a) *Queen Anne's Revenge*
b) *The Bounty*
c) *Hispaniola*

(answers on page 32)

BRAIN BONUS

What was Lai Choi San's nickname?

a) the Chief of the Chinese Buccaneers
b) the Queen of the Macao Pirates
c) the Ruler of the Southeast Sea Dogs

How many shipboard attacks were made in the South China Sea in 1997?

a) 34
b) 67
c) 105

From where were $240 million worth of goods stolen in one attack in 1991?

a) the Black Sea
b) the Gulf of Mexico
c) the Mekong River

(answers on page 32)

THE BIGGER THE BETTER

Even huge ships aren't safe from pirates. In 1991, thirty pirate attacks on tankers were reported in Southeast Asia alone.

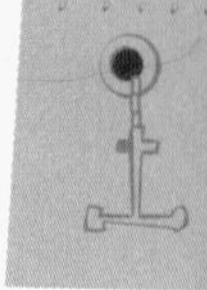

CHINA CRISIS

Piracy was a huge problem in China in the 1920s. Civil war created hardships for many, and some people responded by attacking foreign ships. One pirate leader was Lai Choi San. She made a fortune from stealing valuables and holding people for ransom.

Modern pirates

FIGHTING BACK

Ship captains are warned not to fight pirates if they board. But after the attack is over, naval patrols can be contacted immediately by radio. Radar, helicopters, and aircraft are also used to track down the criminals.

IN DEEP WATER

This photograph of armed pirates was taken in Philippine waters. A group of pirates attacked the British *Seakettle* as the vessel sailed from Sumatra to Indonesia, robbing the crew of valuables before making off in a dinghy powered by an outboard motor.